BY THE SAME AUTHOR

Dusk Before Dawn

LETTERS FROM THE BARRIER

Carys Maloney

Copyright © 2022 Carys Maloney

All rights reserved.

ISBN: 9798404958300

Contents

Letters from the Barrier

The Coward & the Dreamer

Real Ugly Voyage (In Four Parts)

Day Number 28

Art for Art's Sake: A Poem on Nothing but Poetry

The World Is Burning Inside of Our Screens (We Pour Gasoline from the Comfort of a Couch)

The Secret Farm

Wardrobe

funnypoems

Alive and Breathing on Tennyson Down

Know this

Test run: You Are

You Are

Today a Memory Became a Welcome Visitor

Burn Out Blind

Sophie Takes the Stand

All of This Future

Two Poems on Fear

Found page of a Romantic's diary

The Lady Poetry

Abfahrt

Eternity, through the passing moment

A Lament Not Liturgy

Soliloquy in an Empty Earth

Ode no.1: Face Behind the Masks

Sun

What Comes After

Love, all over again

Life Source

Life Source II: Removed

Your right to restart, on the house

Maxim on the nature of Knowledge

On Seeking My Life Lessons from an Oak Tree

The Place of Return

Dismal Residue (or Recently Deleted)

Hindsight (An Excerpt)

Poems in Captivity: Yesterday

Poems in Captivity: 2 by 1.5m

Of Then and Now

Fag end: The immediate future of my unborn children

A writer on writing

Patti Smith Luv Note

We do what we do

In Which I Lay to Rest

...

More Miscellany

Poems for the Cats (after Old Possum)

Nik Beat or An Ode to Liberation in Life and Art

This Is the First Poem

The critic should regard the poem as nothing short of a desperate ontological or metaphysical manoeuvre.

- JOHN CROWE RANSOM

Don't be too harsh to these poems until they're typed. I always think typescript lends some sort of certainty: at least, if the things are bad then, they appear to be bad with conviction.

- DYLAN THOMAS

...Everything I do's been done before
Every sentence in my head
Someone else has said
At each end of my life is an open door...

- JOHN ENTWISTLE

The Coward & the Dreamer

The Coward laughs
at the Dreamer
who dances in colour

Whilst he remains
a prisoner
of the monochrome mind

Real Ugly Voyage (In Four Parts)

NOTICE FOR TRAVELLERS:

A kind of purging. Repulse
A gross dissatisfaction. Abasement

If we could drown our defects in self-pity,
we would never learn to love one another. descend,
we must

descend,

it's kill or be killed out there.
       come again
it's kill and be killed in there.

what goes down must come back up (trust)

................................YOUR BOARDING PASS............................

beyond this
i don't know how all will be.

We collect the years like dust, forget to clean the closet, never mind
the spring, the spring can wait. Stifle the secrets; we're too old
to change that now. skeletons are much less scary with time anyway,
precious antiques; our little brittle companions.
                                                      Ahead, oh
Dread, the Past is like your Bed.

Just watch for them bones 'case they bite your back
is all. Moving on for reals this time:

The epitome of expressionlessness
The craving for comfort
The idea of the moment taken seriously.

Nothing is present nowadays
no options whereby you can experience all
you really learn out on the edge of things

Where the substantial falters on your own terms.
      Shift. If the world fell away under my feet,
it would fail to surprise me. No refunds at this time.

...............TAKE HEED: AN UNFORESEEN INCIDENT..............

Hmpf! Smack down. Ground is the bottom
like rock. The chains take to the chest with peculiar ease.
I am hunched over all that never was.

Time dithers (dimly) by and I
myself am tempted to broach subjects
Foreign yet, to my spoken tongue. In desperation
to rouse Meaning from her all-surrounding slumber,
wake up, sleeping sound, you are sleeping still, still
You sleep—and hearing no sound, so then You squeak:

          In people of all kinds I cannot see myself

There is another way of knowing and recalling—
First, an ecstasy of thought comes your way.

**............DEVOID OF DIGNITY, WE REACH OUR BERTH:
HOLD FAST..**

Moor here, more here, the water is fine, the sea breeze, divine

      My Primordial Passion. And you eluded me entirely
      (O my Blue Flower) So quietly, oh quietly, oh
              Say it ain't so, Joe.

Go, let, go. These waves are not a way station, you know

Drainage issues: seek plumbing help
or spiritual salvation. The water that clogs the chest
And eyes. Layer upon layer or hand upon Hand,
The blanket masks the flesh
and the flesh masks the bone—they bit down
when you searched the closet, what dideyetellya,
bleedin' dust— the kids won't listen —a thing that I say

(they sold me by day, no chance to repay

No refunds at this time.)

Let's go, more to know, we weren't to know

                    we weren't to know.

A light—we alight. I feel now

                                        we   might   be   alright.

Day Number 28

Cat claws and cup rings
emboss the yoga mat
A cardigan of moss green wool

A curious interplay of thunder and rays
presides over the days
The smell of barbeque smoke intermingling with
that of somebody's cigarettes—
Something was said, and ain't that the truth
                and ain't that just so
    Pains in the stomach and stains on the clothes.

Blue and white checks like
                Dorothy's dress—
The juxtaposition of the white clouds against the

            Jagged jewel
            blue sky
fly by, and pallor-stricken pigeons mating on the rooftop again.

                "To every thing there is a season"

& I'm walking through spider's webs
spun at every turn like sticky sushi between
my fingers.

Art for Art's Sake: A Poem on Nothing but Poetry

It happens when I write a poem
I fit my thoughts to rhyme.
I don't know any other way—
I don't suppose you mind.

I could write about anything that
Presents itself to me—
The lonesome leaf, The grain of sand
The latest technology.

You may wonder: Is she so vain
That she sees herself in all?
Or is it a Just Compassion;
An empathy so sprawled?

(The leaf that lingered,
Was trodden to ground—
This may have been me
The next time around

This iPhone 12 is but a grain of sand
For both can be held in the palm of a hand)

They say: There must be rules in play
To keep the Poet in line—
As if the poem were a game;
A trivial passage of time.

Yet where's such order
In this world?—a utopian ideal;

Paddling in the shallows of Life
We are rarely seen to kneel.

So what makes a poem
A poem, after all?
What defines but one single piece?
Rhyme, Stanza, Iambic Pentameter—
Or something that runs evermore deep?

So I say: What is poetry to you?

And that is what it is—through and through!

Yes—all this money
These profits,
that you make

They may comfort you
as a blanket
Protect you,
as a bubble

But if ignorance is bliss
We will reject
such a notion

For it will not revive
Our Eden, from the rubble.

- The World Is Burning Inside of Our Screens
 (We Pour Gasoline from the Comfort of a Couch)

The Secret Farm

Here, here I come again to the secret farm. I've never seen
another person here, though the signs say
it's a public right of way. But I'm not alone, or entirely:
someone has slapped a tree in half and wedged it
inside another—brutish—like a game of Jenga

Something to pass the time.

Ridgeway Farm, it's called. It's secluded and open
and wide and infinite. If you survey the space from atop
The hill, you'll see a red-brick chapel courting
some seven sorry trees in waiting

I could stay here, I think. I walk.

More than before, the world seems exposed
as an Iridescent Mirror; see the stream, and how
it bounces back reflections, always reflections
and evidently reflections

Nothing will try to fool you here.

zzzz zzzzzz zz say the Gnats and Flies—
they're playing out their manic ritual,
a flying frenzy above the forementioned stream
(what makes them swarm like that, I wonder, with no mind
to house a will of their own?) to and fro
they go, they are the people running over
Trafalgar Square, the rain that swaddles the Strand

Last time I came here I saw the woollen Mothers
and their just-born sucklers—those two together,
snuggled up soft like my cats—but today they seem
to be gone, quite suddenly, such a lovely place and
why would they want to leave, I think:

It must have been an alien abduction, bleat bleat bleat,
strange language, or
some suspicious sheep plague, or
that of Man maybe, more likely, maybe
I suppose

I'm walking among the trunks now.

These trees remind me of poised frozen dancers:
branches as arms, extending upward in exuberance,
and with the utmost grace

They have scars on their body, slashed, smiling
(it makes me want to embrace them)
Just as on my inner ankle;

my legs are tree trunks and more beautiful for it.
I think of Japan and Wabi-sabi

Wardrobe

These clothes cling to me
The way you never could
Exasperated. I tear them off—
A preposterous Imposter in
Your place. Soon
I'll be stripping my skin again
Stepping out of me
To observe myself /

The drumroll in
My left rib cage
Precedes what, exactly?

Running through the blue toward
The black;

Sweat on my brow.
A life, in my hand /

funnypoems

i
really wish
that
i
could write
funnypoems

then
people could read
my funnypoems
and laugh
at them and me
probably
which is nice
we would all get
some simple joy

so
it is sad
that
i
cannot write
my funnypoems   just yet. but
                                      i will keep trying
                                      and in meantime

                                      please keep laughing.

Alive and Breathing on Tennyson Down

I

Above the down, nest
groves of golden sunflowers.
From sky above, rest
the winds of another time.
Along the earth, cliff line
jagged and white
Stones break away, then
gather themselves up;

Becoming sane once more.
Butterfly wings flitter by
Clouds elongate,
suppress the sky.
Paths riddle themselves in
messy incline;
Stopping sporadically to observe
one another.

II

If you tread here
Do so with will
Analogous to wind
(For the sordid stone
That lines the terrain
Is condemning, for all
of its beauty)

I try to. Picking, pressing
Four flowers of varying love
Into my denim jean pocket.

III

They say a great poet
Once walked here, too:
*"Stealing by lawns
and grassy plots"*

Carved into cross
Such words are yet lost
So the poetry spans the centuries,
That the poet himself cannot.

But know this—
If the Sun rises only to reveal
A Lone Morning Shadow—there I am.

For the Dawn too, holds a darkness
               at her tail—one we'll so flippantly forget.

Test run: You Are

(You are)
the bait for my brain
the swindler in the game
survival of the sane
the years of mundane
pastimes

Past Times

(You are)
the revolt in my blood
the virility of a flood
my desire from above
the exultation of love's
yearning

(undiscerning)

You Are

(You are)
the incandescent brevity
of day's early light
the ruffle of the feathers
in a dove's fleeing flight

the warmth within an angel's
cries of delight

the eternal oil lamp
to see the Soul
through its Night.

(You are)
the spark within my smile
the truth that's worth its while

the only thing on earth known
to dissipate denial

the hue of midday sky
a friendly passer-by
the mischievous child who
could never tell a lie

the still unbeaten poem
that never made the page
a playwright of baroque declaring
all the world a stage

the reason that I turned
to look Life in the face
can take her by the hand and pray
for heedfulness and grace

(You are)
the missed beat of a heart
that skipped, stammered its part
floundered through a flailing world
and left before its start

Today a Memory Became a Welcome Visitor

I met her with haste
Yet feared her wrath
For I knew I was to be sent
To the grave of a past
That once burgeoned with
Life. Now decaying in vain
So I shooed her away
So as to save me such pain

Yet something had changed
In the way of her greeting;
Armed with comfort, and
Strength (not so fleeting)

And I invited her inside
These confines of a mind
And I surrendered to the glow
Of another place and time.

Embracing her now
We smile and reminisce
How pure it is to
Appreciate, not to yearn
For what we miss

And when she drew back
At last, having alleviated
The past

I found myself able
To let her go

With only adoration
Now left to show

A circle, completed
And a soul, free to grow

For such days may be gone
But their solace, still remains
And how pure it truly is
To recall, in absence of pain.

fin

Burn Out Blind

Cut me open
Pull me apart
You can see for yourself
The content of this heart

The space that is yours
You occupy alone
It gets lonely in there
It's no place for a home

You know more than most
How hard it can be
If you're lost to yourself
Then there's no finding me

Then we're lost to ourselves
Then ourselves we'll debase
Then we're finding new ways

To burn out blind

Sophie Takes the Stand

1.

Slowly, and still in a small voice, Sophie took to the stand and spoke
the following words. She stood, and clasped her hands together,
down and in front of her—both for some moral self-support, and to
keep her nails away from her gnawing teeth, as her mother had said.

But she could not quite muster such Politeness and Respectability
this afternoon—the convulsing blaze in her belly—all fire and
imminence. (And this fire, she knew, that the people needed to feel
it too. But who, in their right mind, would want such a thing?)

At first, nobody took much notice of her.
You could hardly expect them to: nobody could see past
her soft exterior; her body that had not yet breathed ten years
(in April, her birthday was coming up); her slight, stubby hands;
her boyish bob of a hairstyle.

She was no prophet, no venerated sage, no wise old man.
She wore skinnys and a stony expression.

She stammered; stuttered; kept her focus fixed, concentrated and
steady, on a pair of once-white Converse some five feet ahead
of her. *Now, now—or never!*

She stammered; stuttered; unleashed an inaudible sigh, and her
willpower—so great just this morning—took this airy outlet as an
opportunity to escape her, abandon her, from her mouth now, away.
Not now, never. No!

Foolish girl! she thought: *What a fool you are
to have tried to tell them, something you do not even know yet
yourself.*

(She was no prophet, no venerated sage, no wise old man.)

And so, resignedly, Sophie stepped down from the stand.
Really, no words were spoken on that day at all. Nada.
Not by Sophie.

So the town bells struck two in a malice of laughter.
So the world resumed its garrulous game.

2.

Face meeting the Ground; a pavement's cooling kiss. Sophie
pitched: *Swallow me up, I'm spice and all things nice.* But the
Ground was stuffed from gobbling her pride; Iblis dosing up
on sin.

Face stinging, chest churning, and with loose laces Sophie made
herself scarce, stumbling and falling flat on her tear-laden face. Only
when she settled herself on an aching wooden bench at the back
of the town, did the following thoughts swim, swim to the surface
of her cleansed, salty consciousness—fashionably late, as ever—
which was still beaten up with shame:

We've consented to lose our Humanity to procedure,
we should've read the T&Cs. Accept and proceed
Are you sure, you are not a robot? A warm hug,
a sincere smile, and we wonder where
It all went wrong;
We know nothing of our own hearts,
our brains are much too full.

In her shame, it made Sophie smile. The sentiment seemed familiar
yet forgotten—the black and white TV, the man with the voice that
had fled her. But the thoughts were not yet done—and then:

What if we turned ourselves inside out
and had a staring contest? It could be a little uncomfortable
at first, but the stores would go bankrupt.

Never mind—what we need,
it is in here somewhere.

In here somewhere. Yes! she had felt it—if only for a moment,
that fire did flicker, and she knew: it was in the others too. Those
ones back in the town, they held this same scorching truth—
a kind of wisdom fire—all those

Who she could not bring her gaze to meet, nor her words, alas,
she could never, never make them see. But they themselves—
they themselves could. For her, on her behalf, for themselves,
each one must realise it through themselves, that which is important.

And in a foreign land, someone Sophie would come to love very
much, found themselves nodding in agreement.

She was no prophet, no venerated sage, no wise old man.
Not yet a saint; not a holy man.
Yet the same thing that these ones nurse within them, and proclaim
without them, she too, Sophie, had it; and now she knew, despite
her tears, lack of years, face of fears—and the rest.

She spat out her nail, tied her laces, and scuffed her shoe on some
gum.

All of This Future

I thought that nothing
Appealed to me
But it seems
This no longer
Stands true

Restricted, was my
Field of vision
To only the things
I knew

Turning, tossing thoughts
Over themselves
Beats a brain up
Black and blue

The buzz of a brain
With nothing to gain
But then, again
Nothing to lose

Two Poems on Fear

1. Side note: Fruit

and I could not bear for anyone else
to feel afraid, that way—

Oh! How I wanted to take such Fear
And make a Fruit of it. Yes—
I'd chop it up into bite-sized chunks

And Consume it myself. Poison Fruit.
Then I'd leave it to transmute

In a stomach pit of despair.
Dissipate like the devil,
Who was never truly there.

2. Rest Well in Your Light

Whatever strikes fear
Within your heart
Cast it aside
To wallow in dark

To wither in dark
Fear cannot grow
If deprived of attention;
This Light of your own

Deserves to dwell
On things much higher
Deserves to expose
The fear as liar

So next time fear
Feigns to bite
Stay soundly in Knowing;
Rest well in your Light.

Found page of a Romantic's diary

dreams are ~~futile~~ fertile

The Day's immature vanity can be likened only to
the flippancy of Reason—evading Love's nightly caress
of depth. We are the enthralled.

A sticky velvet sky sodden
with screaming stars. Watch over the Lovers;

                      the moon undressing the ocean

                          again. sway and shine, a kind of

                              seduction. calling out like

a black watery death

The Lady Poetry

I'll voice my
Words into
Verdant life;

They'll split through
The air, pierce
As a knife;

They'll scorn over
Treetops, ridden
With vice;

They'll drape me as
Clothing; they'll
Surely suffice;

They'll make me look
Anything, but
Passive and Nice.

Abfahrt

The late-train retreats, languid and slow,
Crawling away a caterpillar. The white cat
Streaks the street right to left, dissecting a cul-de-sac
In half-dark; lampposts shine their presence,
Amber and pink, soft: Rhubarb & Custards.

The sight is sweet, the night
An echo on the train's tail,
Out of view now from the onlooker
Above the evergreens. So peace is found at the end
Of the day, a much-awaited détente
From the trials of sunlit shenanigans;
To surrender to sleep now would be a sin, surely
You can see this—

But, no—sirens, stark and shrill, and
I'm in another time—crippled in apprehension.
What is real, what is real? To touch
Something—to affirm my existence here
In safety. An anchor: metallic and manifest.

Eternity, through the passing moment

the past and the pain
they start to dissolve
a mind lost of memories
and stories untold
this process unfolds
so i may experience

               peace
the freedom in presence
and the joy
in release

A Lament Not Liturgy

Tonight I do not want to sleep
Tonight the night is mine to keep

Inside my thoughts are not my own
Inside the Source remains unknown

They say that now
Is the time to weep
I guess they commanded
My Fall so deep

To you, I am: Always
Almost there, and
You're all that was—
Ain't life unfair?

He will never give you
More than you can bear
So rest your mind;
So do not despair.

Perhaps I will lie
Beneath the trees
Perhaps I will learn there
How to concede

(The Source will spring up
Naked and alone
Startling, Oblivious
Unchanging in tone)

He will never give you
More than you can bear
Sound it to the stars;
Recall it in a prayer.

Perhaps I will lie
Beneath the trees

Wax and Wane and Rot and Seethe
Pass through the years on a comical breeze;
Stop here and there, alight as I please.

Tonight: I do not want to sleep.
I will tuck myself into
Our throbbing heartbeat.

Soliloquy in an Empty Earth

You have (1) new message from (1) unrecognised number. New message:

```
''Are you there?

It's been a little while.


Might you picture something for me?
```

It felt as if I were living in a metaphor for loneliness: caught in some flimsy spider's web of fragile hopes, extending out from one core, so full of life, and then diced down in a single sigh of unforgiving wind...

Streets were wracked with defeat, ransacked of defiance and any picture of a prosperous full future—so crudely defaced by the circumstance of the present (need I say anymore?) that presented itself to this beating body...

And so real seemed all of this that it is what I too became—you know how sensitive I am to my surrounding, acute, and in ways imperceptible to others. So this vengeful void that forced itself upon me—and I think now of love and light and other inextricable entities to you… I hope you know only joy and kindness, consistent with all that you are. Hot, slow tears—and so apart from this unspeakable place, I shall leave you in that sought-after one.

My thoughts are trains: frequently departing but never arriving. *(Aside) The doors got jammed on the Circle line.*
I myself seem altogether lost in transit— and all these silly metaphors for that matter. Decked out in disguise… I hope you laugh. How we complicate things by thought!— though it's likely you can tell,
you discern me, all too well.

I feel deeply, how I have been bitten by the recent passage of time—the clocks with their tick-tock! hands and teeth and nails, how they drag me under their sovereignty, and that which we make, makes us its slave—and yet I hold a stubborn hope that I may come back one day. Plentiful and laughing with cotton candy hair… as I once was, yet stained with experience turned wisdom. If only some lasting warmth would lead this loved one out from her burrow—a firm hand grip and not letting go now—for venturing out alone into this empty shell of an earth she is sure to be banished back, to the banal (Eurydice, Eurydice), as we have witnessed, over and over and over within a year past. *(Aside) Oh, Virgil! Dante showed us: Hell is circular.*

Where, was I? To ponder is painful, yet it is
a shallow existence without.
Is it a time that marks a place, or a place
that marks a time? A place a place, a time a
time alone, no… the subjectivity that moulds
everything into a basking bliss or vacant
abyss.

Now. An unreal struggle has stated itself—
back to what we know. So
if we can cling to our best self—or the best
we can keep from slipping back to heaven—
I think that is how we are to survive.

And survive, is what we must do.

It's easier said than a mind undone.

The last thing there is to say.

I remember I had a dream—I can't be sure when
exactly. But I was holding your hand and your
life within that hand, and we were in a blue
sky with big fluffy clouds, and I looking
down, I couldn't see your face, and I did
not know you. And then something took you
away from me

I remember your hand falling away from me

I think I'm nearly home now, but something strange up ahead. No matter.

I'll leave you with your favourite line, though in full knowledge of the inadequacy of words:

Let all things end as letters: the last word being your name.

Yours, as always

Sole (Soul) Survivor''

Sent 12:26, Earth A, date unknown.

! To save this message, press: (1)
To delete this message, press: (2)

Ode no.1: Face Behind the Masks

To the young girl who dwells
In the corner of the room
Eyes downcast, shy
In avoidance of life's gloom

To the boy who bounds and
Bumbles—smile stretched from
ear to ear;

A second of pure enchantment
Shakes a reality screaming
so near

To the woman who
Dreads the dawn,
A stomach of sobs forlorn

To the man who
Never knew why,
A clench of tears yet cried

To all of the lovers scolded
By those with the minutest
of minds

Let it be known:
That which is shown

                Is never and cannot be
                a life, in its entirety

And these people you pass
Still distorted by masks

                              The plays of a past,
                              that no one dared see.

(we are crazy enough to believe
we are sane, in a world where a smile
shrouds a lifetime of pain)

Sun

i have come to believe
that the scathing sun
has found its home
within my chest.

imploding,
relentlessly
scolding a beating
heart into ashes

the heaviness
of this light
never does fail
in making itself known.

What Comes After

Sometimes, desperation
wears your old facade thin
When the sorrow is not coming
from the outside, and in

There seems no safe haven
in which you may reside
You ponder if you can outrun
what has chosen to live inside

You're sure others see you
standing, all alone
but they can't see through
you;   the interior of a mind

Where a battle still belittles
Unforgiving, deep inside.

This fight for yourself—
It's the toughest thing
you will ever have
to endure

(I am certain there is
no one thing, that could
threaten to test you
anymore)

So believe me when
I say, that soon
Shall come a day

where the time
does slow

and the pain
does fade

Breathing again, once more
notice the air tasting sweet
A phoenix from the ashes;

truly risen
from defeat.

And suddenly, I realised
It never mattered
To me—
If the day that you call me
And love me
Right back
Is a day that I should
Never get to see.
For I shall love you—
Regardless
Sincere
Completely

However you may choose
To live out your days
Even onward and
Ahead now,

without me.

- Love, all over again

Life Source

Being alive
is not in the breath
being alive
is connection—
To places to people
to Self to love
To abundant unanswered
questions.
The same way survival
is not distinct from death
for death is found
as isolation—
Removed from reason
from hope from love
From a line beyond this
comprehension.

Life Source II: Removed

you never wanted
to be the recluse
but it seems, circumstance
grants little other choice
you wanted to run
to utilise your voice!
in a singular reality
should you welcome
with rejoice

yet instead you are mourning
a life you'll never live
just a yearning in a dream
this world could never give

cruel ambition—desire
that is keeping
you alive

                                shred your attire of bondage!
                                      all such figments—
                                           folly. lies

1x blank page* date of expiry: N/A

[valid for: 1x 'fresh start' or 'blank slate' **ONLY**]

*simply pretend these words were never here.

Maxim on the nature of Knowledge

It should be known that Intellect and Ignorance are not by any means mutually exclusive.

On Seeking My Life Lessons from an Oak Tree

Stood before
the Great Oak Tree
I am conscious of my own
Insignificance.

Armed with modesty
and tenderness, I make my approach
Toward her roots
Looking for a hint as to how
I too, might remain as grounded
if only through the passing seconds
let alone the innumerable decades
she has succeeded
In her Still and Silent triumph.

Sat beneath
the Great Oak Tree
I am looking for the secret
of peaceful Indifference.

In her trunk
Stands not a trace of unrest;
~~She does not revolt like these~~
~~Fibres within me~~
~~That wear themselves thin.~~
~~Exhausting petty conflict.~~
Her only movement,
a celebratory number:
we know it as the
brief union with breeze,
that passes, as surely

as the Days the Nights
Cries of Birds in Flight
the Fading of Light
the Laughter the Lives
and all of these things
that mark the backdrop
of Time

As she
the Great Oak Tree
remains unaffected
despite this fact

The white noise of the world
then becomes a soundtrack
Serenading her stance:

Unwavering, Unmatched

The Place of Return

Flowing on. The days become one another and
I submit myself to them, making our roots
The same; I submerge myself in them,
not to be unearthed

Nor revived. Here is the place
In which there is no space
No face, no other, nor divide

We melt and mingle, no thing left single
A consummation (like sex) thus betides.

Dismal Residue (or Recently Deleted)

And so, it happened
On hitting the ground
Knees tucked to chest
I was, of sort
A bomb: defused and delicate.

And then, on seeing
Your sad sad smile.
Something screamed, in the
Sedatest section of sentience
(A seed yet realised
Flowered Fresh and Fertilised
Within your Light). And so then
It began, and so now
It continues

Until my form changes once more.
Until I shed my futilities, demanding
"No more".
Until, once more, inexorably
I meet the floor:
Legs failing, flailing, mangled and raw.

For, I cannot fly here
Nor may I dance—
Yet seeing through this
Silver tether of romance

Demands that the blue
Bathe my eyes, once more
Aborting decaying depths
We'll wade through closed doors

(And be met with applause)

And so, it happened
On hitting the ground
Knees tucked to chest
I was, of sort
A bomb: defused and delicate.

Hindsight (An Excerpt)

Yet there was never going to be
An easy way to see:
The loss of what you never had
Is a gain, in that it sets you free

And only in hindsight do we
Laugh or Sigh or Scream
For it is all so much clearer now
Alive, at age eighteen:

The truth that we must first
Wake from sleep, in order to live out
The life of which we dream.

Poems in Captivity, 1/2

Yesterday

Then, there came a day—
He no longer looked to
The stars. Eyes of glass
Vacated—smashed
He lay atop his scars.

The body becoming
A burden. The mind
Becoming a slave.
The walls, becoming
His impenetrable cell

For such things rarely change.
She doesn't know
How to rouse him.
She's unsure
Of what she may find

For who can say
Just what demons play
Within the forsaken mind.

Poems in Captivity 2/2

My bedroom is measured at 2 by 1.5m

I've outgrown it in more than one sense
Of the word. The walls are dark
Saturated with secrets, with eyes that
Avert in modesty—shy with sights that
Paper could never bear the weight of.

My bedroom is measured at 2 by 1.5m;
Each night I rest with a body spanning the perimeter—
In bed, a head that holds the wall, and feet that meet
The opposing side. Wardrobe is white, stained, straining.

I stand before the mirror like a bruised Barbie in a box;
a woman on display;
as the world looks on through the window.

Do not pity me; it may be a cell, but I paste
my essence on these walls.
Make it my own—what God knows
I've outgrown. Each night
I'm as restless as the shivering silver alarm clock;
ticking through time and space as I complete
Another round of days—the calendar—
crossed seven times per week.

Do not pity me, I beg: as I sleep, as I weep
for I soar, in schemes not so concrete-based;
as I permeate my space—a seraph
Fallen and Incarcerated, lays down to waste

In a bedroom that measures at 2 by 1.5m

Of Then and Now

I think, I shall start
Tomorrow. Then:
When the weather is fresh and favourable,
When the sky plucks its feathers blue.
And I shall feel just the opposite.

I think, I will start
Today. Now:
When the rain is real on my skin.
When the air is heavy in my lungs,
And I, feel just as weighted—
Yet Here I am.

Fag end: The immediate future of my unborn children

it was all once there
but alas
now it's gone—
that is, the lives
we could have had
so what on earth
went wrong?

well they did not stop to think
sleeping a world
over the brink
and it's a real shame
a true loss—
you really think
they give a toss?

—of a coin, as to
our making it out
even then, an
earth to hold us? sad
i largely doubt

for they are big on up
with plans for mars

if they could only first save
what remains
under these stars

then we might stand a chance—
but inconvenience of circumstance

so turn the other way
and drift on,
day to day, to month
to year to—*Oh!*
Well where did the time go?
Looking back at my life
Now, and what have I to show:

The children I love
Are drawing hands up above
And praying for time
Or a miracle, sublime

Their future—more bitter
Than my Glass of Red Wine.

A writer on writing

To preserve all things
that else, flee away;
To make them real
To make them stay.

- Why write?

I don't really know
if my words are any good

(I do not even know
what 'good'
is supposed to mean)

So maybe when I write
it is only in vain
but the words will remain

And remain,
all the same.

- So you call yourself a Poet?

Patti Smith Luv Note

Ms. Patti Smith,

I can not rite 4 myself anymore - my self a ghost shaded in solepsism. And so I will write 4 u & all that you do And also do not do. Take last week I saw u at Royal albert Hall and sang and cried a lot bc of the words you spit and songs u writ and all of the people u drew on I felt them there with us as One just like you said. Mostly though I cried bc I heard truth spoken out loud. and saw a woman at ease all free and thats all I want to be & funny I made it there now goin so far to go nowhere atall. I smiled wide whn U ripped up yr guitar like broken lyre strings of soul set free or else bad poem like this one.

So here is my luv note 4 u Patti after gr8 beat up poets Peter n Allen. plz never change never stay the same & rite for all the wrongs in the world. Now i would hit send bt im scarred of the intanet. has no real substance howcan it exist......wierd but still god maybe. Any way. let me put in print to touch is much beeter i think these days.

all my adoration

anon

We do what we do

Until we don't anymore.

It works until it doesn't

And then we must change

In Which I Lay to Rest

I did my living through dreams, then through handheld screens.
Now, Life herself beckons me back—and with a gesture as gentle as
a mother, escorting her firstborn across a virulent crossroads.
Protecting them from the upheaval of oncoming engines, lurching,
stalling, leering,
preying

The light shows green. Ten seconds on the clock. Stepping out
alone, my wrist recoils; I lead you on with your heart without ever
touching your hand. I'd have liked to have done nothing more. But
see the Path approaching and now the number four. Three.
Pavement stretching out stubborn, anticipating my footstep—two.
The things I wish I knew, oh, *the things I should have done.*

But I shall not succumb. Amber

One

the way is not in destruction, but rather in creation.

pessimism is the final untruth.

More Miscellany

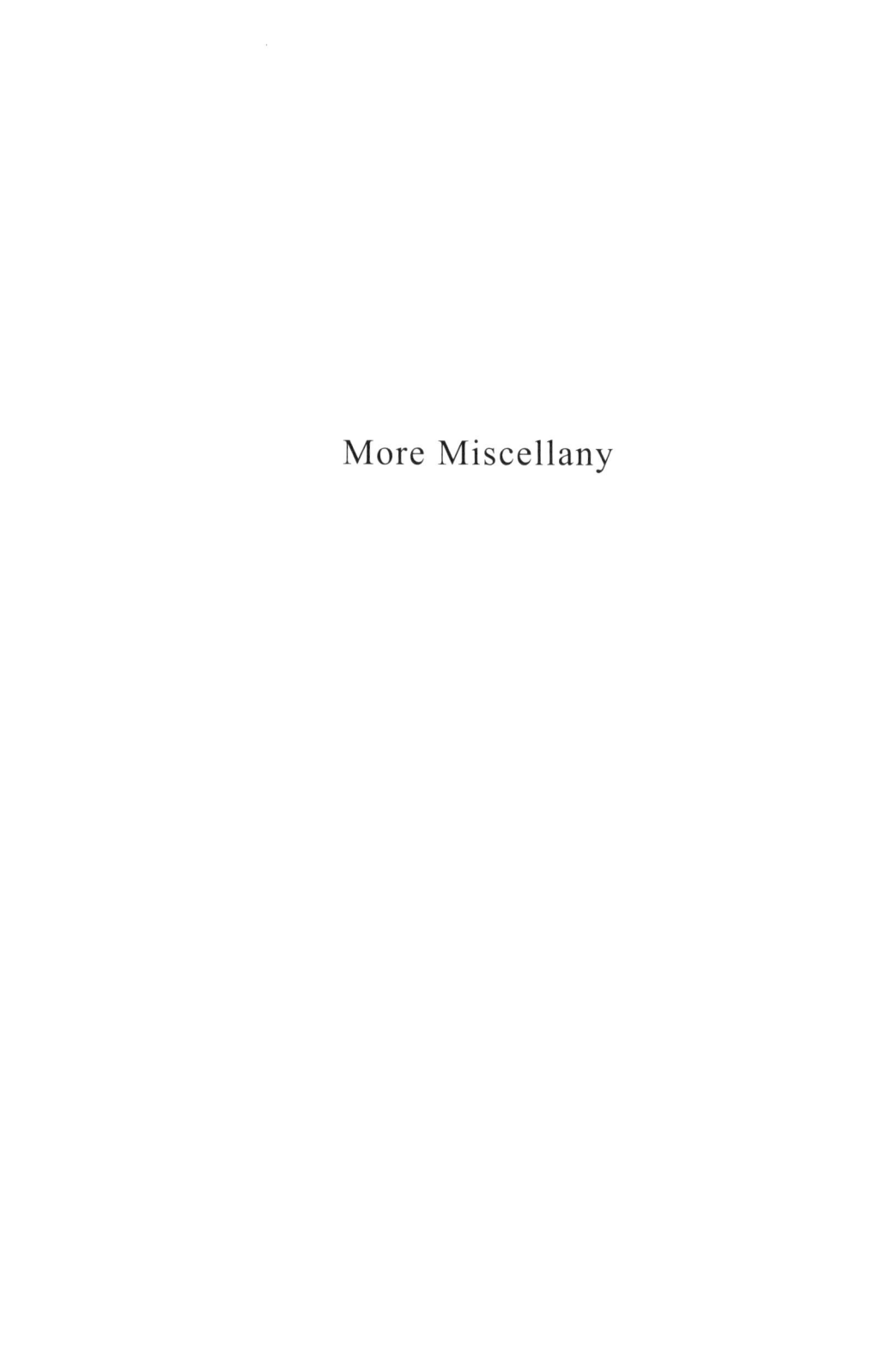

Poems for the Cats (after Old Possum)

1. The Scabby Cats

Griff and Bella: The Scabby Cats!
They are sure to lift your mood.
You'll find them in the garden room
Eating their Kitten Food.

Now both of these furry felines
Are known to love a brisk brush.
And when the time for tea is here
(Meow!) Carys can get no hush!

Exploring when the summer arrives
That's the way of Griffy—
And though he's been known to travel afar
These days, he'll be back in a jiffy!

He loves to cuddle and snuggle right up
Pink-nosed; the smoother of the two.
And if you see him sneak into the house
Well—that's nothing new!

Bella will jump and leap and straddle
An athletic kitty, no doubt.
She'll look at you with large doll eyes
Then sneeze—and yawn—and pout!

But in the night, these two do fight;
They let their mischief run loose.
Yet by the day, they'll even play
Or put their paws to use,

By taking a (cat) nap on the couch
Deep in sleep, they'll purr—

And when they think that Carys can't see
They'll clean each other's fur.

Bella and Griff—so now you know
These Scabby Cats and their ways.
Black and white, siblings by sight
They'll wreak havoc within your days!

2. Fancy Nancy

Fancy Nancy! The little one;
She's certainly very small.
A charming coat of many colours
She is loved by one and all.

She'll dart and dash, this way and that
Right across the hall!
She'll roll and flop all over the shop
Then off the sofa, she'll fall…

Dreamies and Tuna—delicacies of choice
The finest for our Nance.
Queen of the house, she will make sure
That all do respect her stance.

Griff and Bella may make their approach
But alas, their effort, in vain—
For Tiny will chase them back outside
Though soon to be seen again!

Now Nancy is an eloquent cat;
Oh, she can hold a conversation.
And when Carys gets out her suitcase
She'll curl up inside for vacation!

Alert and afraid, she may run and hide
Upstairs, in Carla's room—
Yet in the evening she's in the lounge
Near the radiator, she'll loom.

So that's Nancy, the fancy feline
With Carys as her mother.
It has been noted—she's a cherished cat
Like her, there's surely no other!

Nik Beat or An Ode to Liberation in Life and Art

Keep ripping, gentlemen! This is a battle—a war—and the casualties could be your hearts and souls! Armies of academics going forward, measuring poetry—no! We will not have that here.
- DEAD POETS SOCIETY

Let us write like kids! In keep with the Beats
Freedom of Expression shun Convention
surly sheep   Let words bounce off our Breast
Pithy shot & neat   Might punch us outta sleep
like some Pacifist Poet Preach

    No Feat   No Feat   No Feat
Put my heart where it belongs at your feet   I can't sleep
a week can't stand in Heat   Gotta keep me aBreast
    I'm outta sorts   In Real Deep

Poets ALL MY POETS May Your Light Never Dim

Tagore mon Amour   with   Donne my English Son

&

Keats

Questionable ½ poems wedged
Bedraggled linen sheets
                  (should I keep?
Rimbaud Fell to Hell with
Dante   when
Jack and Jill went up
The Hill—Creeley
Inferno inferno inferno deep

I wanna sing like the Beats cos
Culture coma deep   At 32
Corso writ mit so much wit
And Pure—Never to Kerouac
I'd show the door—Orlovksy won
the spelling bee he never had to work
no more—found Burroughs flee US for
Mexican tequila Cantina cat (I ain't sure about that)
Junky New Orleans, San Fran &
                                New York
Patti wrote Witt genstein sip coffee napkin scrawls

Audre who was Voice wrote in Strength spoke by Choice

VU & Lou Reed gone way up to Mars no
Kansas City Bars   just yet.

Let us don our words as Sustainable Dress!!
Proclaim our stupor souls An Imminent Caress let us digress

profess
          confess

     our unrest

Of our silly selves let's show our mess!
Then our best—or not
Love what we have let us want
what we got   And when it's got
Beat Up real shot
Let's let it go go go   go

Our stupor souls Words don as Clothes
Naked Lunch Bill Burroughs   let us
Dine without wine, Five and dime
I'm through with this life in the light
in the lime
Let us write without lines and laugh in the margins.

It's too hot today I'm all razzled inside
Frazzled. Melt a melody sing ablaze
In Cafés   America's Dazzled
O Hara O Hara
Brooklyn baby Lana

But I'm Welsh like Thomas who
Blessed the Chelsea 205 NY
City Manhattan street. memories of holidays
and sand that strews the feet Too young
our Young Dog braved the tide of Porthcawl
Coney (Island) Beach

Poets ALL MY POETS May Your Light Never Dim

Amy Jim my Soulful Kin

Poets ALL MY POETS May Your Light Never Dim

Won't let 21st cent cash you out on its Whim
(insta poetry in-thing   3G-4G-5G Fling
Playing with the Page in days when
TikTok weren't a thing) when Dylan writ abhorring
Vietnam WAR IS OVER IF YOU WANT IT

WAR IS OVER   RAW IS LOVE

Tear up the margins   spew souls   sporadic speech
I wanna long live the Beats drizzle revelation overleaf
rail receipts

This Is the First Poem

This is the first poem I've written in a year.
You see, I was in Heaven
And they have no pens or paper there—besides
My memory is bad. In truth
I write my poems in my iPhone notes
But that died before I did, so
I left it behind. Anyway
I haven't written for some time now.
And there's no time in Heaven
at all, which certainly
does not help my case.

In Heaven, you see
There's nothing to say. Instead
Everything is known—rightly understood.
Thus the language of the word is rendered obsolete.
No one to communicate the bliss of one's exalted state.
On the surface of the Earth does the word retain its worth.
Yes. But I was deep, asleep
Properly tucked up and buried.
That's another thing we got wrong about Heaven—

It's a kind of falling, a downward movement
The cessation of strained flight. Week after week
My watch failed to speak.
No one mentioned I'd still have two feet
brown hair   twisted spine
Ceremonial heartbeat. Everything looked just like Earth
like a snow globe shook up a landscape rebirth.

I floated around my body my mind thefalseideaofmyself
and rejoiced as the snow settled them down to dirt.
The globe still shaking I was still
I was waking. I held the hands of clocks and sang
Ring-a-Ring o' Roses until they all
                              fell
                                 down
with me
deeper, still, deeper.

Resistance brought me back here, an aeon
of restless tendencies. Back in time disregarded divine.
Remain undisturbed the return to written word.

                              (I woke up this morning with
                                 my pockets full of posies.)

For a far-off land, it really wasn't so far
After all. I don't recall
How I got there, but I hope
I get back one day. Somehow
I think we all will—it's too familiar a place.

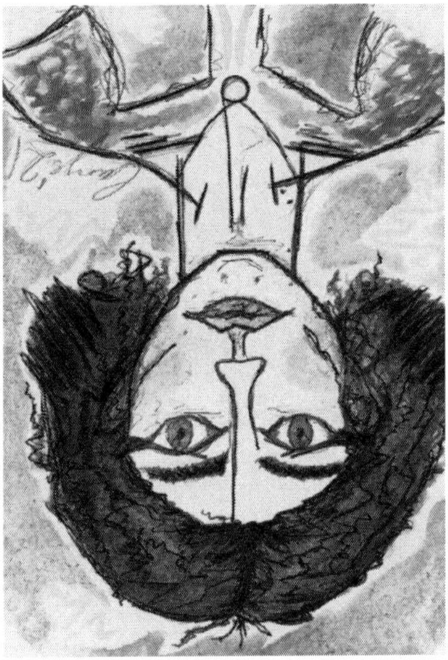

Printed in Great Britain
by Amazon